The Christmas Pony

Laura put her arms around Mr. Crumbs's neck and hugged him. "I've decided what I'm going to do. I'm going to raise the money to keep him myself."

"How?" asked Ben.

"There are lots of ways." She kissed Mr. Crumbs on his soft nose. "I won't let you be sent away to strangers. They won't know where you like to be scratched or what your favorite treats are. I'm going to find a way to keep you — somehow."

The Christmas Pony

SYLVIA GREEN

Illustrated by Sharon Scotland

SCHOLASTIC INC.
New York   Toronto   London   Auckland   Sydney
Mexico City   New Delhi   Hong Kong   Buenos Aires

For Mr. Crumbs — and Rosie
And for Laura and Emily

ISBN 0-439-44928-6

12 11 10 9 8 7 6 5   3 4 5 6 7/0

Printed in the U.S.A.   40
First Scholastic printing, November 2002

Chapter 1

Mr. Crumbs

"Of course you can't have a pony for Christmas, Laura. We couldn't possibly afford one." Dad looked determined.

"But it's not just any pony — it's Mr. Crumbs," said Laura. "And he's free to a good home."

"Ponies cost a fortune to keep," said Mom. "And apart from that, we've got nowhere for him to live."

"We'd find somewhere —"

"No, Laura," said Dad. "You know how difficult things are at the moment."

"But if we can't give him a home, he'll have to go and live at the horse and pony sanctuary," said Laura. "We'll never see him."

"I'm sorry, but the answer's still no," said Dad, in his don't-you-argue-with-me voice. "It's just not possible."

He went back out to the garage to finish the oil change on Mr. Robert's Volvo, and Mom went to answer the telephone.

"Told you they wouldn't agree," said Ben. "It's not practical."

Laura spun around to face her brother. "Oh, why do you always have to be so — so sensible?"

"Probably 'cause I'm older than you."

"Only one year," said Laura.

"Dad's been really worried about money since he was laid off," said Ben. "Especially since he had to take out that big bank loan to start the business."

"I know, I know — I had noticed," said Laura. Dad was always in his garage these days, repairing cars for people or out chauffeuring wedding parties in his vintage Rolls. And Mom spent most of her time in her workroom, making wedding dresses. "But there must be something we can do."

Laura marched out of the room feeling angry and frustrated. She couldn't just give up. She put on her coat and headed for the front door — a visit to Mr. Crumbs always made her feel better.

She set off down the lane and soon spotted Mr. Crumbs. He was across the field, socializing with the goats on the other side of the fence. He loved company. His sharp hearing immediately picked up Laura's footsteps, and he raised his head and gave a loud whinny. With his ears pricked, he trotted over to her.

The late November sun shone on his golden coat — it was the color of toast crumbs, hence his name. Mr. Crumbs was a palomino pony — his pale mane and tail contrasted beautifully with his golden coat. He had a white blaze on his nose and a white stocking on one of his hind legs.

Laura closed the gate behind her and smiled up at the pony.

"Hello, Crumbs." She stroked his warm broad forehead, but he immediately tried to push his large nose into her pocket, eager to find out if she had something for him.

Laura laughed as he nudged her. "Easy. You'll knock me over." She took out the ready-sliced carrot and gave him a piece.

He watched her with his velvet-brown eyes as he crunched on his favorite treat. Then he tilted his head and peered out of the corner of his eye to see if she had any more carrot in her other hand. Ben called that his "quizzical look."

Laura laughed and gave him the second piece. "There's no fooling you, is there!" She loved the feel of his silky-soft muzzle on her hand as he quickly searched out the carrot and gently took it. Mr. Crumbs never failed to cheer her up, but this time she couldn't help feeling a little sad.

"I'm afraid Mom and Dad said no," Laura told him, as she patted his firm shoulder. "But don't you worry, I'll think of a way to keep you."

Mr. Crumbs tossed his head, shaking his long mane, and blew gently through his nostrils. Laura couldn't imagine life without him. For as long as she could remember, he'd been there in his field. They passed him on their way into town and on their way to school. At first, they'd just stopped to talk to him every day and sometimes have a chat with Mrs. Cox, his owner.

Gradually, they'd spent more and more time with him. Then a year ago, Mrs. Cox had been ill, and Laura and Ben had helped look after Mr. Crumbs. When Mrs. Cox was better, they'd continued to help, and in return she'd taught them both to ride him. But now Mrs. Cox was moving to Australia to live near her daughter, and a shopping center was going to be built on her land. She had to find a new home for Mr. Crumbs before she left.

"Mrs. Cox says no one will buy you because you're too old," said Laura.

"I don't think you're old — you're only eighteen. You could easily live until you're twenty-five."

She reached up to scratch him on the

head, under his forelock, and Mr. Crumbs bent his head toward her. Next to carrots, his favorite thing in life was a good scratch under his forelock.

She heard the gate click and turned to see Ben.

"Hello, Crumbs," said Ben, reaching up to pat him on his glossy neck.

Mr. Crumbs greeted him with a soft whinny.

"Mrs. Cox says they're very kind at the horse and pony sanctuary," said Ben. "And he'll have lots of company."

"But it's miles and miles away. We'll never see him," said Laura. "I thought you wanted to keep him, too."

"I do." Ben adjusted his glasses with his free hand. "You know I do — but I can understand why we can't."

Tiggy, Mrs. Cox's cat, strolled over to

them, and Mr. Crumbs put his head down to greet her.

"He's going to miss Tiggy — and the goats — as well as Mrs. Cox," said Laura. "I can't bear the thought of him missing us, too."

put her arms around Mr. Crumbs's
and hugged him. "I've decided what
I'm going to do. I'm going to raise the
money to keep him myself."

"How?"

"There are lots of ways."

"Such as?"

"Oh, lots and lots of ways — I'll think
of something."

She kissed Mr. Crumbs on his soft nose.
"I won't let you be sent away to strangers.
They won't know where you like to be
scratched or what your favorite treats are.
I'm going to find a way to keep you —
somehow."

Chapter 2

The Mr. Crumbs Committee

"Emily says she'll help me raise the money," said Laura. "And she's offered to help look after Mr. Crumbs."

"What does Emily know about looking after a pony?" said Mom. "I know she's your best friend, but this isn't a game. It's a big commitment."

"She knows that," said Laura. "She's come with me to visit Mr. Crumbs lots of times and she loves him, too. I'll teach her how to look after him."

"Emily's mom won't have any money to spare for a pony," said Dad.

"I told you. We're going to raise the money ourselves," said Laura. "Emily's coming over in a minute to discuss it."

"All right. You find out how much it costs to keep a pony," said Dad. "Then, if you can raise enough money in advance to keep Mr. Crumbs for at least six months — and find somewhere to keep him — we'll think about it."

Laura was overjoyed. Things were looking hopeful. But as her parents left the room she heard Dad whisper to Mom. "She's just a kid," he said. "She'll never do it — not six months' money in advance. We're quite safe."

"How dare he call me 'just a kid,'"

Laura complained to Ben. "And how dare he say I'll fail before I've even started."

"No, that was unfair," said Ben. "It even made *me* mad."

"Then why don't you help us?" said Laura. "Let's prove to Dad and Mom that we can do it. We can own Mr. Crumbs between the three of us — you, me, and Emily."

Ben took his glasses off, polished them on his sweater, and put them back on again. "Well, I suppose we could just do a business plan and see if it might work."

"A what?"

"A business plan. Like Dad did when he was setting up the business. It's what all good businesspeople do to see if their ideas are practical."

"But we're not a bus —" Laura started, but quickly stopped herself. Maybe it was a good idea — especially if it meant that Ben would help. . . .

As soon as Emily arrived, they all sat down at the kitchen table.

"This is so exciting," said Emily, shaking back her long dark hair. "I can't believe that we might own Mr. Crumbs by Christmas."

"Now hold on — don't get too excited," Ben warned her. "It might not be practical. It's a pretty big thing, owning a pony."

"We can do it," said Laura. "I know we can."

"Well, the first thing is to see if it's possible," said Ben. He had just put his calculator on the table and opened his notebook when there was a knock at the back door.

Ben's friend Sanjay popped his head around it. "Hi! You ready to go, Ben?"

Ben jumped up. "Sorry, Laura. I gotta go. We're going to ride our bikes."

"You can't leave yet," said Laura. "We've only just started."

"Started what?" said Sanjay, shutting the door behind him.

Ben explained about Mr. Crumbs.

"Don't you want to keep him?" asked Sanjay. "I think it would be great to own a pony."

"It's not that I don't want to keep him," said Ben. "I just don't think it will work."

"Well, I'd certainly want to give it a try if it were me," said Sanjay. "I've always wanted to have my own pony."

Laura thought quickly. "Would you like to join us, Sanjay? It'd be better with four people — cheaper for all of us."

"Wow! That'd be amazing," said Sanjay, grabbing a seat and drawing it up to the table. "Imagine — owning Mr. Crumbs."

"Terrific!" said Laura. "Let's get started." Another advantage of Sanjay's joining them was that there were now three different families involved. If any of them were on vacation — or ill — there would always be someone to look after Mr. Crumbs.

"I thought we could call ourselves the Mr. Crumbs Committee," said Laura.

"Great," said Emily.

Ben opened his notebook. He wrote THE MR. CRUMBS COMMITTEE and listed their names. "We need to work out how much money we think we can raise and how much it will cost to keep him. And don't forget we haven't got much time. Mrs. Cox is moving just after Christmas."

"Christmas is only four-and-a-half weeks away," said Emily.

"Exactly," said Ben.

They started by discussing their pocket money. Laura and Ben each got two dollars and fifty cents a week. Emily got two dollars and Sanjay got four dollars a week, because he helped with recycling all the packaging at his dad's drugstore.

After some discussion, they decided it would be fair if they each put one dollar a week into the fund. They would all need some money for themselves — for Christmas presents, sweets, and CDs — and Ben was saving up for a computer.

"Okay, fund-raising," said Laura. "I thought car washing — we might get some business from Dad's clients."

"Dog walking," said Sanjay.

"Shopping," said Ben.

"Snow shoveling," said Emily.

They all looked at her. "But it's not snowing."

"It might. If it gets a bit colder," said Emily. "I love snow."

Ben wrote it all down. "We could

18

charge two dollars for everything we do. Keep it simple."

He quickly worked out that if they each did one job a week — for two dollars — and each added the one dollar from their pocket money, the total among them would be twelve dollars a week.

"That should be plenty — surely," Laura said.

"Well, the next thing is to find out how much it will cost to keep Mr. Crumbs," said Ben.

"There's his food," said Laura.

"Vet bills," said Sanjay.

"Bedding?" said Emily.

"And rent — if we can find somewhere to keep him," said Ben.

"What about the field where Maggie keeps her goats?" suggested Sanjay.

"That's been bought up for the shopping center, too," said Ben. "Maggie's moving down South and taking the goats with her."

"We'll soon find somewhere else," said Laura.

Ben listed everything. "When we've found out all the information, we'll be able to see if it will be practical."

Laura smiled to herself. Of course it would be practical. It was going to work out — she just knew it was.

Chapter 3

Making Plans

Later that afternoon, the four friends met up at Mrs. Cox's, and Laura gave Emily her first grooming lesson.

Mr. Crumbs loved being groomed. He closed his eyes and gave a low snicker as Laura worked over his neck with the brush.

Laura smiled. "That's his favorite part."

22

"He's gorgeous," said Emily, patting his glossy shoulder.

Laura showed her how to brush Mr. Crumbs's beautiful mane and tail with the body brush. She brushed each of his legs and then gave him a drink of water.

The pony looked up expectantly as Ben arrived with his feed bucket. He pawed the ground impatiently until it was given to him. Sanjay carried the hay bale, and the two boys hung it up in the stable.

Mrs. Cox arrived with mugs of hot chocolate for them all. "I'm thrilled to bits about your plans to keep Mr. Crumbs," she told them. "I do hope it works out. I'll be much happier knowing that I'm leaving him with people he loves — and who love him."

She didn't think it was impossible at all. Laura and Ben had proved how well they could look after Mr. Crumbs during the past year. The only thing she insisted on was that they all had their parents' permission and that they found a good stable to keep him in — with supervision from an experienced adult. "However capable I know you are," she said, "I'm afraid I can't just hand Mr. Crumbs over to you."

As they sipped their drinks, they watched Mr. Crumbs munching intently in his large bucket, sorting out the carrots to eat first. Gradually an orange, slobbery mess formed around his mouth.

Laura chuckled. "That's why I leave washing his muzzle until last."

"Good thinking!" said Mrs. Cox, laughing. "Now, you asked about the cost of keeping him. I've done a few quick calculations. There's his feed mix, vitamins, hay — oh, and his carrots." She smiled at her pony's orange lips. "We mustn't forget his carrots. So, all his food, and straw for his bedding, adds up to about ten dollars a week."

Ben whipped out his notebook and wrote it down.

"Then there's his shoes."

Laura sighed. They'd forgotten about shoes. It was already going to cost more than she'd thought.

"Mr. Norris comes every six to eight weeks and does them for me for forty-five dollars," said Mrs. Cox.

"Forty-five dollars?" said Emily. "Every six to eight weeks? Why?"

"It's very important that Mr. Crumbs has new shoes and his feet trimmed regularly," Mrs. Cox explained. "Otherwise he could get sore feet, or even damage them."

"Oh, I see," said Emily.

"Then there's vet bills," Mrs. Cox continued. "Including worming, vaccinations, and having his teeth checked regularly. It's difficult to put a figure on that; it depends what needs treating at the time."

Ben tapped away on his calculator. "Food, bedding, and shoes comes to approximately eight hundred and thirty-five dollars a year. That's about sixteen dollars a week. Plus, we need to put something aside for vet bills."

"We're only going to have twelve dollars," said Emily. "It's not enough."

Laura sighed, but she wasn't going to be discouraged. "We can do two jobs a week each," she said quickly. "That'll bring in another eight dollars."

"Two jobs is the maximum," said Sanjay. "We've got to leave time to see to Mr. Crumbs and do our homework. And don't forget I have to help my dad, too."

"Two jobs each brings it up to twenty dollars a week," said Ben. "We'd be okay for his keep — and probably the vet bills. But there's still his stable. We don't know how much that's going to cost."

"I'll ask around for you," said Mrs. Cox. "I'm sure we can find somewhere nearby to keep him."

"I do hope so," said Laura, gently washing Mr. Crumbs's nose and muzzle with a sponge.

Then Ben untied him, led him into the stable, and took his halter off.

Tiggy immediately jumped up onto the stable door. Mr. Crumbs came over to greet the tabby cat, and she rubbed herself against his nose before jumping down and settling in the straw.

"Mrs. Worth at the post office has offered to take Tiggy in," said Mrs. Cox. "But Tiggy and Crumbs are really going to miss each other."

Laura wondered if they could find a way to keep them together, but she didn't say anything — not yet.

Mrs. Cox picked up the empty mugs. "If there's anything I can do to help, let me know," she said and headed indoors.

Laura and Ben picked up a shovel and a bucket.

"Okay," said Ben. "Now for the fun job! We've got to pick up his droppings from the field. We have to keep it clean."

"Manure!" cried Emily.

"Er — yes, Emily," said Sanjay. "That *is* what it's called."

"No, silly. What I mean is — my Uncle Jack buys manure from the garden center to put on his garden," said Emily. "And so do lots of other people. We could sell the manure to raise money."

"Great," said Laura, laughing. "What do you think you can manage, Mr. Crumbs? A bucketful a day?"

Mr. Crumbs tossed his head and walked over to his hay bale.

"You've embarrassed him now," said Sanjay.

Ben was taking notes. "We could probably get between twenty-five and fifty cents a bucket for it," he said. "I bet we could earn one or even two dollars a week. Well done, Emily, that's a great idea."

Emily beamed at him.

"We need to think up more ideas like

that," said Sanjay, as they headed for the field. "Our biggest problem is going to be raising six months' money up front. We haven't got much time."

Laura thought about it as they went about their task. It would be difficult, since Mr. Crumbs needed a new home shortly after Christmas. There were only four-and-a-half weeks to Christmas, and if they were lucky, they might have one or two weeks afterward.

"What we need is a big money-making idea," said Ben.

"How about putting on a Christmas show?" Emily suggested.

But the others didn't really like her idea — they thought it would be too complicated.

Then Laura had a brainstorm. "A Christmas bazaar!" she cried. "We can make things — and collect stuff from other people to sell."

"That's a great idea," said Emily, as they hurried back to the stable. "I bet we'd make lots of money."

Mr. Crumbs heard them come back and put his head over the stable door to join in the conversation.

"We'll need somewhere to hold it," said

Sanjay, patting the pony's neck. "A hall or something."

"Halls cost money to hire," said Ben.

"It needs to be somewhere cheap," said Laura. "Somewhere cheap — and different."

"Something like a big shed or a barn?" asked Emily.

"A barn would be great," said Laura. "We could decorate it and make it really Christmassy."

Mr. Crumbs tossed his head and gave a little whinny. He obviously agreed.

"That old man next door to you's got a barn," said Sanjay. "D'you think he'd let us use it?"

"I dunno," said Laura. "But it's worth a try." Mr. Jakes had lived next door to them for about six months, but they hardly ever saw him. His house was a converted farm cottage and in his backyard was a big old barn that had been on the land when he bought it from the farmer. He sometimes said hello to Mom or Dad, but he always seemed very unfriendly toward the children and avoided them whenever possible.

"I can't imagine he uses the barn for anything," said Laura. "And surely for a good cause like this . . ."

"We'll go and ask him tomorrow morning," said Ben, "once we've looked after Mr. Crumbs."

Chapter 4

Mr. Jakes

"I'm not usually up this early on a Sunday morning," said Emily, yawning, as they put the stable-cleaning equipment away.

Laura smiled. "You'll get used to it."

They started down the driveway and paused by the gate to the field. Mr. Crumbs was concentrating hard in his efforts to pull the hay out of the hay bale they'd hung up for him. He swung his head around to them, chewing thought-fully.

Laura scratched him under his forelock. "Your stable's all done, so we're leaving now. See you tonight, Crumbs."

Sanjay stroked him. "Doesn't he get cold out here?"

"No, his coat is nice and thick, and it hasn't been clipped," said Ben. "But if it gets really cold, we put a blanket on him."

"Oh, right," said Sanjay, as they left. "Well, Emily, we've had our first lesson in mucking out."

"Yeah, we're learning fast," said Emily. "I'm so glad my mom said it was okay for me to own him with you three. Even if she did agree with Ben and Laura's dad that we had to get at least six months' money up front."

"My mom and dad were actually quite

excited," said Sanjay. "They said the responsibility would do me good."

"I'm really glad they agreed, too," said Ben. "If this is going to be possible, it'll need the four of us."

"Of course it's going to be possible," said Laura. "Now come on, let's go and ask Mr. Jakes about his barn."

There was no answer when they knocked on Mr. Jakes's front door.

They tried around back, but there was no sign of him there, either.

"He's probably gone out," said Sanjay.

"Let's have a quick peek inside the barn," suggested Emily. "We might be able to see what it looks like."

They had just reached the barn when the door opened and Mr. Jakes came hurrying out. "What are you kids up to?" he shouted.

Ben, Emily, and Sanjay all jumped back, but Laura stood her ground. "Good morning, Mr. Jakes," she said. "We were — er — just wondering if we could use your barn for our Christmas bazaar."

"I don't want kids around here, causing trouble," said Mr. Jakes, hastily pulling the barn door closed behind him. "Go away."

"But —"

"There's nothing here to interest you. Don't come near my barn again."

"What an unfriendly man," said Emily, as they hurried away.

"Why's he so touchy about an old barn?" asked Sanjay.

"Maybe he's a bank robber," said Emily. "And he's got all his loot stashed away in there. He looks like a crook — he's got shifty eyes."

"Well, we've got more important things to worry about than him," said Laura.

"Such as where else to hold our bazaar — and where we can keep Mr. Crumbs," said

Sanjay. "Obviously no point in asking Mr. Jakes if he can live in his barn."

"Wouldn't be any good, anyway," said Ben. "Mr. Crumbs needs at least an acre of field to run around in during the day."

"There must be lots of other places," said Laura. "Like — like the farm next door. They must have another barn if they sold this one to Mr. Jakes."

"Okay, we'll go and ask," said Ben.

They trudged next door, trying to remain cheerful. But the farmer didn't have a barn they could use for the bazaar. And neither did he have any land he could rent out for Mr. Crumbs to live on. Even Emily's offer of free manure toward the rent couldn't sway him.

They went home for lunch. It wasn't a very good start to the day, but they all had fund-raising plans for the afternoon. Sanjay had arranged for him and Ben to wash his dad's car for two dollars. Emily was going to walk a neighbor's dog. And Laura had offered to do some housework for an elderly friend of her mom's.

They agreed to meet afterward to turn Mr. Crumbs in for the night and to discuss how well they did.

Laura was the first to arrive. Mr. Crumbs immediately left his powwow with the goats and trotted over to her. She slipped the lead rope around his neck and gave him a piece of apple.

"Good boy," she said, as she slid the halter over his nose. She lifted the strap behind his ears and buckled it up. "You're such a good boy."

Laura walked alongside his head and

led him over to the stable. "We haven't found anywhere to keep you yet — but we've got lots more ideas," she told him.

Tiggy greeted them outside the stable, and Laura got the grooming kit. She took out the hoof pick and ran her hand down Mr. Crumbs's front leg to his fetlock. He obediently lifted his foot so she could pick out his hoof. "I wonder where the others have gone," she said. "I'm dreading telling them how much I earned this afternoon."

Laura had finished grooming Mr. Crumbs and was giving him his drink of water by the time Ben and Sanjay arrived. They held out four dollar bills. "We washed two cars," said Sanjay. "One of my neighbors saw us washing Dad's car and asked us to do hers as well."

"How much did you get, Laura?" Ben asked.

It was time to own up. "Ten cents."

"Ten cents?"

Laura explained how she'd cleaned the lady's whole kitchen, including the oven. Then the old lady had thanked her and given her ten cents. "I don't know if she didn't hear me properly or if she didn't have any money," said Laura. "But I didn't want to ask for more."

Ben laughed. "Let's hope Emily did better." He went off with Sanjay to get Mr. Crumbs's food.

But Emily arrived with no money. The dog she was walking had run away, and she'd had to get the owner to help find it. So, of course, he didn't pay her.

Ben did a quick calculation while Mr. Crumbs noisily searched out the carrots in his bucket of food. With the one dollar contribution each from their pocket money, they had raised eight dollars and ten cents. "We've got a long way to go," he said.

Laura sighed. "Let's go home and start figuring out what we can make for our bazaar."

"Okay," said Ben. "We'll have a meeting of the Mr. Crumbs Committee on Wednesday evening and see what we've all come up with."

Mr. Crumbs finished his food, and Laura washed his nose and orange lips with the sponge. "Don't worry, this is only the first weekend," she whispered to him, as she led him into his stable. "There's still loads of time."

He gave a little whinny and she was sure he understood her.

Chapter 5

We Can't Give Up

They had a half day of school on Wednesday so Laura seized the opportunity to take an extra ride on Mr. Crumbs. During the winter, she usually only got to ride him on weekends, because it got dark so early.

Emily was doing some shopping for an elderly neighbor, and Ben and Sanjay were chatting with Mrs. Cox. Laura liked her time alone with Mr. Crumbs. She gave him a gentle squeeze with her legs. "Walk on, Mr. Crumbs."

He obediently set off around the field. Somehow the field, and the surrounding area, looked different from between Mr. Crumbs's ears. It was as though she were seeing it from his view.

She gave him another squeeze. "Trot on, Mr. Crumbs."

They trotted around for a while and then slowed to a walk. Mrs. Cox was happy for Laura to exercise Mr. Crumbs on her own. She knew she could trust her just to stay in the field. Laura's riding hat had been a birthday present, and Mrs. Cox had given Laura and Ben riding boots that had belonged to her children.

Laura brought Mr. Crumbs to a halt. She leaned forward to pat his neck. "That was great. Good boy." She slipped her feet out of the stirrups and dismounted.

"We're having a meeting of the Mr. Crumbs Committee tonight," she told him, as she ran the stirrups up the stirrup straps. Then she slackened the girth. "Ben wants to talk about his business plan, and we're going to discuss our ideas for the bazaar."

She led him off toward the stable. "But we haven't found anywhere to hold the bazaar yet. The village hall is much too expensive — and in any case it's booked. And so are both the church halls."

Laura tied Mr. Crumbs up and took his saddle off. "But the rest of the fund-raising's going quite well. Ben washed one of Dad's client's cars yesterday, and I cleaned the inside. We got two dollars each. Sanjay earned two dollars for cleaning his dad's store window, and Emily should get two dollars today."

Mr. Crumbs tilted his head, peering out of the corner of his eye to see if any food was coming yet.

Laura loved it when he did that. She laughed and gave him a carrot. "We've already found a customer for your manure," she said, as his soft lips searched her hand to make sure he didn't miss any bits. "Emily's uncle. And he knows lots of other people with gardens."

Sanjay arrived and said that Ben had gone straight home to work on his business plan. He helped Laura groom and feed Mr. Crumbs and clean the riding tack. Then they headed home, both looking forward to the meeting that night.

Ben spread his papers in front of him on the table. He took his glasses off and polished them on his sweater. "I don't think we can do it."

"What?" Laura looked at him in horror.

"It's just not practical," said Ben, replacing his glasses. "Mrs. Cox has been asking around and she says the very cheapest stable we're likely to find — just a field and basic shelter — is ten dollars a week."

"Not that she's found any that are available," said Sanjay. "And neither have we."

"Therefore, with ten dollars a week for food and bedding, six dollars toward shoeing, two dollars — at least — toward vet bills, and ten dollars for the stable, if we can find one, that makes twenty-eight dollars a week," said Ben. "We can't earn twenty-eight dollars a week."

"But that's twenty-eight dollars among four of us," said Laura. "Seven dollars each."

"I can give an extra dollar a week," said Emily. "Mom got a raise, and she said if I keep my bedroom clean and tidy, she'll give me another dollar a week pocket money."

"And I don't mind making my contribution three dollars," said Sanjay. "Since I get more than the rest of you."

"Well, I'm perfectly happy to give two dollars a week from my pocket money," said Laura. "There's nothing I want to spend my money on more than Mr. Crumbs."

Ben wrote it all down and reluctantly agreed to raise his share to a dollar fifty. "That makes eight dollars and fifty cents a week," he said.

"And the manure," said Emily.

"Okay, let's say an average of a dollar fifty a week for the manure," said Ben. "So that's ten dollars a week plus what we earn."

"And at two jobs a week each that's another sixteen dollars," said Laura. "So that's twenty-six dollars a week — we're almost there. We could make the bazaar an annual event to raise the rest of the money."

Ben did some more calculations. "We'll need to make at least a hundred and four dollars profit from the bazaar every year. But don't forget we've got to raise the first six months' money in just a few weeks. That's about seven hundred dollars. I just don't see how we can do that."

"Oh, for goodness' sake, let's at least try!" said Laura. She ran up to her room and came back with her piggy bank. "I was saving for a new bike, but I want Mr. Crumbs more." The coins clattered all over the table as she shook it.

Ben counted it out. "Twenty-seven dollars and sixteen cents."

"I'll ask for money for Christmas instead of a present," said Laura. "And for my next birthday. And I don't care how hard I have to work. I don't want anything except Mr. Crumbs. We can't give up."

"I don't want to give up," said Emily.

"No, let's give it a little longer," said Sanjay.

"All right," said Ben. "We'll keep trying for a while. I suggest we keep the money in a savings account at the bank. At least it will be earning some interest."

"Good idea," said Laura. "Now what about the bazaar? I've got my list of ideas here." She took out a piece of paper. "I thought we could cut out gift tags from old Christmas cards and make tree decorations — I've seen some ideas in a magazine. Make fluffy spiders and chicks out of old wool, and have a Guess the Number of Candies in the Jar competition."

"Great," said Emily. "Me next. I thought of making fudge and coconut ice cream —

Mom's got some really easy recipes. Making grab bags — we can buy some cheap little gifts from the market and wrap them up. And we could sell refreshments."

"I thought of painting some ordinary cheap pots to plant bulbs in," said Sanjay. "And I could make paperweights, plaster models, and table decorations."

"And perhaps you could design some posters to advertise the bazaar, Sanjay," said Ben, "since you're the one who's best at artistic-type things." Then he got out his own list. "Christmas cards," he read. "Buying up large boxes from the market and cutting them into nice smaller packages. And doing the same with wrapping paper. And we could sell secondhand books, videos, and CDs that we can collect from friends and neighbors."

"Great," said Laura. "And perhaps Mr. Crumbs could give pony rides."

"Good idea. We could charge fifty cents a ride," said Ben. "I'll make a note of all the ideas and how much we could charge."

"There's only four weeks until Christmas," said Sanjay. "So we'd better get a move on."

"Yes. This has got to be the biggest and best bazaar ever," said Laura. "It's got to make lots and lots of money."

Chapter 6

More Ideas

On Saturday morning, Laura and Emily met up to see to Mr. Crumbs, while Ben and Sanjay delivered manure to the gardens. Mrs. Cox usually took care of her pony on weekday mornings and the children came every evening after school and twice on weekends. Soon — when Mr. Crumbs belonged to them — they would have to get up early to take care of him before school as well. Laura couldn't wait.

Mr. Crumbs pawed the ground, impatient for his feed. His warm breath rose like steam in the morning air.

Emily finished brushing his tail and wiped under it with a sponge. "It was a shame about Marsham Hall, wasn't it?" she said.

"Yes, I'd really got my hopes up about that," said Laura, as she gave Mr. Crumbs his feed bucket. Marsham Hall was a big house just outside town, and the owner kept three horses of her own. "Such a pity she didn't have room for Mr. Crumbs as well."

They'd also tried Church Farm, Westdene Farm, and Mr. Brown, who ran a market garden — but they didn't have any luck there, either.

Emily giggled as she watched Mr. Crumbs searching out the carrots in his bucket. "I love the way he does that," she said. "He's a real carrotoholic."

Laura smiled and patted the pony's warm neck. "I hope Ben and Sanjay have some luck at the vet's when they've finished delivering the manure. A vet must have somewhere to keep large animals that need shelter."

"Yes, and if not, they're bound to know of somewhere else we can keep him," said Emily. "They must know all the farmers around here."

Laura led Mr. Crumbs out to his field and filled his hay bale and water trough, while Emily started cleaning out the stable. On Saturday mornings they removed all the straw and disinfected the floor.

As soon as they'd finished, the two girls

made their way to Fowler's Family Restaurant. Sanjay's mom had suggested they might have a room the children could use for their bazaar.

"I'm really sorry but I'm using the room for extra seating now," said Mr. Fowler. "But I think it's great what you kids are trying to do. When you do find somewhere, I'll give you a voucher for a meal for two as a raffle prize."

"Wow, thanks," said Emily.

"Why don't you try the Rose and Crown Inn?" he suggested. "They've definitely got a banquet room they rent out."

But the landlord of the Rose and Crown Inn couldn't help them, either. "We have got a room," he said. "But I'm afraid it's fully booked for Christmas parties until the end of January."

It was disappointing, but encouraged by the offer from the restaurant, Laura summoned the courage to ask if he would consider donating a raffle prize.

"I'll give you two bottles of wine," said the landlord. "You'll have to get your parents to pick them up, though."

"A raffle's a great idea," said Laura, as they left. "You make lots of money with a raffle."

On the way home, they stopped by the hardware store (the owner said he couldn't give them anything) and then the vegetable stand (the counterperson promised them a basket of fruit).

As they arrived at Laura's house, Emily spotted Mr. Jakes carrying two large boxes of "loot" into his barn. "Did you see the shifty way he looked around him? I bet he *is* a bank robber. Hey!" Emily grabbed Laura's arm. "D'you think there might be a reward for his capture?"

"A what?"

"A reward." Emily's eyes were shining. "Just think, it would solve all our money problems for Mr. Crumbs."

"Oh, Emily, Mr. Jakes couldn't possibly be a —" Laura started, but Emily wasn't listening.

"We ought to spy on him — see if we can get any evidence." Emily crept over to the hedge to peer through. She turned back suddenly, her eyes wide. "Hey! I just heard someone crying out. It came from the barn."

"Honestly, Emily, your imagination gets worse all the time," Laura giggled. "It was just a chicken. There are tons on the farm. Now come on."

She ushered Emily indoors, and they found Ben and Sanjay in the kitchen looking through the ads in the local paper. They hadn't had any luck at the vet's, but the vet said they could advertise for somewhere to keep Mr. Crumbs on his bulletin board.

"We thought about putting an ad in the paper as well," said Ben.

"And in my dad's drugstore window," said Sanjay. "And the post office."

"Great," said Laura. "Let's write some out after lunch."

"We've got to make ourselves a sandwich," said Ben. "Mom's doing a fitting for two bridesmaids in the living room."

"They must be the ones in red velvet," said Laura. "Mom was working on their dresses yesterday."

They heard the steady chug of Dad's

vintage Rolls as it pulled up in the driveway. He'd been chauffeuring a wedding
over in Stanton, about twenty miles away.

Dad opened the kitchen door. "You kids
couldn't do me a favor, could you? Wash
and polish the Rolls? I've just driven down
a really muddy street and the car's filthy."

"How much?" asked Laura. This was
business, after all.

"Five bucks, if you can do it right away,"
said Dad. "I need the car for another wedding at three o'clock, and I've got to fix
Dr. Johnson's BMW."

"Oh well, lunch will have to wait," said
Ben, as they filled buckets with hot water
and got old cloths. They started work on
the muddy exterior, and Laura and Emily
told the two boys about the raffle prizes.

"That's great," said Ben. "I've been
working on the numbers for the bazaar.

63

The packets of gift tags we've made should sell for fifty cents each." He wiped the water splashes off his glasses with his sleeve. "So that's eighteen dollars if we sell all thirty-six packets. And the fluffy spiders and chicks could bring in twenty-five dollars — if we can make fifty."

Emily giggled. "Only if we can make the chicks look less like vultures."

"Tonight we ought to wrap up all those notebooks, pencils, and plastic toys we bought at the store for the grab bag," said Sanjay.

"And we should start on the big boxes of Christmas cards," said Laura. "I thought we could put twelve in a packet and maybe stick tiny crepe-paper bows on the front to make them look nice."

The car was soon washed and dried.

The boys polished the exterior, while Laura and Emily started on the big chrome headlights.

Then they swept the confetti out of the interior and put fresh white ribbons on the front. It looked good when they'd finished. Even Dad was pleased — and he was very fussy.

"You've done a really good job," he said, handing a five-dollar bill to Ben.

Laura watched him reverse the car into the garage and had an idea. Dad's garage was big — not really as big as they wanted, but it could work. "Dad, as you're out most Saturdays at weddings, could we use the garage for our bazaar?"

"No, Laura. Even if I have two weddings, like today, the car is back here at some point, and I need to keep it in the garage," said Dad. "And there's usually a customer's car in there, too."

"Shame, the garage would have been good," said Sanjay, as they went indoors. "But at least it's lunchtime now — at last."

As they ate, they wrote out the ads for the vet's, the local newspaper, Sanjay's shop, and the post office.

"What about the library?" said Sanjay. "They've got a bulletin board."

"Yes. And they might have a room for the bazaar," said Laura.

"Let's go there first," said Ben. "There's only three-and-a-half weeks to Christmas now."

Chapter 7

A Breakthrough

Laura paused from sifting out the soiled straw with the fork to watch Mr. Crumbs. Emily was sitting on him and Ben was leading her around the field.

He's so beautiful, she thought. *We've got to raise the money to keep him.*

They hadn't had any luck getting a room for the bazaar at the library yesterday. But they had put up one of their fly-ers asking for a field and a stable.

Mrs. Cox knew when she was moving out now — the eighth of January. So they had to find somewhere for Mr. Crumbs to live before then.

Laura sighed and went back to sorting out the straw. "Hey, watch it, Tiggy," she said, as she spotted the tabby cat curled up in the corner. "You don't want to be put on the muck heap, do you?"

Tiggy reluctantly got up, stretched her-self, and strolled outside.

Laura wheeled the full wheelbarrow around back and had just put the fresh straw in the stable when Ben brought Emily back on Mr. Crumbs. Laura held the pony's reins and stroked his nose while Ben helped Emily to dismount.

There was such trust in Mr. Crumbs's

velvet-brown eyes as he looked at her. "I won't let you down," she told him.

Laura took her hard hat from Emily and swung herself into the saddle.

She walked Mr. Crumbs back to the field and leaned over and patted his strong neck. "There's still time to raise the money," she whispered to him. "And to find somewhere to keep you."

She gave him a gentle squeeze with her legs. "Trot on, Mr. Crumbs."

They had a busy week. Every evening, after they'd taken care of Mr. Crumbs and ate dinner, the four friends met up to work on things for their bazaar. But they still couldn't find anywhere to hold it.

Laura was glad when it was Friday — she was looking forward to spending time over the weekend with Mr. Crumbs. She and Emily waited for Ben and Sanjay after school as they usually did, so they could all go together to tend to Mr. Crumbs.

But the boys were late coming out, and Laura was getting impatient. "Where are they?" she asked Emily. "We've got to take care of Mr. Crumbs and sew the legs on all those fluffy spiders for the bazaar."

"They didn't say they weren't coming with us," said Emily.

Laura sighed and went back into school to look for them. She was tired — they were all tired.

She spotted Ben in the hall. His class was performing a Nativity play for the rest of the school, and they were obviously rehearsing.

Ben saw her and came to the door. "We'll be about another half an hour," he said. "You'd better go on without us."

"Why didn't you tell me you had a rehearsal?" Laura demanded. "Emily and I could almost have finished tending to Mr. Crumbs by now. And we've got loads more work to do this evening. There's only two-and-a-half weeks to Christmas now." She felt so tired, and her head was beginning to ache.

"Sorry," said Ben. "I forgot."

"You forgot?" Laura snapped. "The trouble with you is that you don't really care, do you? Oh, you come along and do a few bits and pieces. And you write numbers in your notebook. But you're not committed, are you?"

Laura didn't wait for an answer — she stormed out of the school to where Emily was waiting for her.

Emily did her best to cheer her friend up as they walked along to Mrs. Cox's, and Laura had calmed down a bit by the time they got there. But Mr. Crumbs always sensed when Laura wasn't happy. Emily was fixing the hay bale in the stable, and Laura went to untie the lead rope to take him inside.

Suddenly, Mr. Crumbs brought his head down and rested it on her shoulder. She reached up and stroked the side of his face. His warmth and familiar smell were comforting.

The two girls paused outside Laura's house, and Laura even managed a smile when Emily spotted a ginger cat going in to Mr. Jakes's garden.

"I wouldn't go in there if I were you," Emily told it. "He'll probably eat you — or make you into fur gloves."

"Emily, that's awful." She giggled.

Emily left to go home for dinner and Laura went indoors and straight up to her room. It was full of things they'd made for the bazaar, as well as secondhand books and CDs they'd collected from friends and neighbors, and a Christmas cake Emily's mom had made for them. Ben had decided they'd make more money from the cake if they asked people to guess the weight rather than just sell it.

They'd got a jar of candy for people to guess how many there were. And The Bookstore had given them a book coupon for the raffle.

Laura slumped down on the bed and looked at the stacks of boxes. What was the use of it all if they didn't have anywhere to hold the bazaar? For the first time, she felt really discouraged.

The door opened and Ben came in. Laura ignored him — she was still mad.

"How about holding the bazaar in the school hall?" he said. "And for free?"

"What? I mean — how?" Laura wasn't sure she'd heard right. "You're not joking, are you?"

"No." Ben adjusted his glasses. "I thought about things after you'd left. And how hard you'd worked — it's all down to you, really."

"Look, I'm sorry — about what I said," said Laura. "We've all worked really hard. I was tired and — oh, just tell me what happened."

"Well, I knew the school hall is only used for school events," said Ben. "But I thought it was worth a try, and I told Miss Featherstone all about Mr. Crumbs."

"And she said we could use the hall? Just like that?" said Laura.

"Not quite 'just like that,'" said Ben. "She was impressed with what we've been doing — and she just happens to love horses. So she made a couple of phone calls and then came back to say it was all okay — for Saturday, the fifteenth of December."

Chapter 8

Busy Days

The next day, Saturday, was really busy. All four of them spent the whole day working on things for the bazaar. But none of them felt tired anymore.

When they went to bring Mr. Crumbs in for the night, Laura and Ben left Emily and Sanjay to groom and feed him on their own while they cleaned up his field.

Both Emily and Sanjay were quite competent now, and the pony was happily sorting out the carrots in his feed bucket when Laura and Ben returned.

"We've definitely reached a turning point now," said Sanjay.

Laura nodded and patted Mr. Crumbs. "Bet you anything someone will call this weekend and offer us a field and a stable."

"Yeah — for practically nothing as well," Emily chuckled.

Mr. Crumbs finally lifted his nose out of the bucket, and Sanjay gently washed it with the sponge.

The pony had picked up on their excitement and looked from one to the other. Then he tossed his head and whinnied.

Ben laughed and patted him. "It's great, your moms' offering to make the refreshments for the bazaar," he said to Emily and Sanjay.

"Yeah, they got together this morning about it," said Sanjay. "My mom's making lots of different treats and Emily's mom is making cakes."

"And they're going to serve tea and coffee and orange juice," said Emily.

"That's great," said Laura, but she felt a little awkward. Emily's and Sanjay's moms were helping, and Sanjay's dad was donating a box of bath products for the raffle. But her mom and dad hadn't offered anything.

Dad had been chauffeuring a wedding today, and she'd hardly seen Mom. The two bridesmaids with the red velvet dresses — and the bride — had arrived in the morning for a final fitting, and since then Mom had been shut away in her workroom. They were both obviously too busy to help.

Emily started to lead Mr. Crumbs into the stable, but halfway there he resisted and turned to look at Laura.

Laura patted him. "Go on, Crumbs. Emily knows what she's doing."

Mr. Crumbs obediently went inside, and Emily took off his halter. She closed the half door on the stable behind her, and he hung his head over it so that he could be included. He hated to miss anything.

Mrs. Cox arrived with their hot chocolate. "I'm so excited about your bazaar. It's really looking like you might be able to keep Mr. Crumbs now," she told them. "Oh, I know the sanctuary would take good care of him, but I'd much rather he stayed with you."

Laura smiled at her. "Thanks."

"I only wish I could help you out financially, but all my money's tied up in the move to Australia," said Mrs. Cox. "But if you'd like any of the tack — saddles, bridles, that sort of thing — you're welcome to it. And all the stable-cleaning equipment."

"Wow, thanks," said Laura. "That'll be a terrific help."

The next week was spent in a frenzy of activity. They worked like crazy to finish the things they were making. Mrs. Cox was clearing out her house and getting ready to move, and she gave them more books and lots of knickknacks to sell. Emily's uncle promised them produce from his garden and some plants from his greenhouse.

There was no doubt about Ben's commitment now. He spent hours making Christmas decorations to sell. He made bells, angels, Christmas trees, and robins, which he cut out of cardboard. Then he painted them, covered them in glitter, and threaded string through their tops.

Laura and Emily bought dozens of hyacinth, crocus, and daffodil bulbs from the market and planted them in Sanjay's brightly painted pots.

Sanjay painted banners and posters to advertise the bazaar. They put them up everywhere anyone would allow them to, including three in the school. He also painted some large stones with brightly colored patterns, to be used as paperweights.

They all made table decorations out of logs and holly, and Emily made fudge and coconut ice cream. Laura and Ben wrapped up another fifty grab bags. They decorated a large box with crepe paper and filled it with shredded newspaper to hide the gifts.

On Friday evening, everything was packed up, and Sanjay's dad drove the stuff to the hall. "Looks like this will take two trips," he said.

Then Emily's mom arrived to take Emily to pick up the raffle prizes they'd been promised.

Laura and Ben's dad was still in the garage, and their mom was in her work-room — she'd hardly come out all week.

Laura and Ben called out to them as they left. "We're going to the school now." But they didn't come out to say good-bye.

Miss Featherstone was waiting for them at the hall. She seemed quite excited as she helped them carry in the boxes. "I can't believe how much stuff you've got," she said.

The janitor had already put out tables for them, and Laura immediately started arranging Christmas cards and gift tags on one of them.

They'd just finished unloading Sanjay's dad's car when, to everyone's surprise, Laura and Ben's mom and dad showed up, too. Dad's car was piled up with the rest of their goods.

Mom and Dad unloaded everything from the car and helped arrange it on the tables. Just as they finished unpacking the last of the goods, Mom handed Laura a large box.

Laura opened it to see six dolls dressed as brides. Mom had used the leftover material from all the wedding dresses she'd made. Under a layer of tissue were eight soft Santas made from the leftover red velvet from the bridesmaids' dresses. So that's what she'd been doing all week.

"Oh, Mom." Laura flung her arms around her mother. "Thanks."

"And this," said Mom, handing her an envelope. "It's a voucher for your raffle. I talked Dad into giving a free ride in his Rolls."

Laura was overjoyed. Everything was going so well. Then an awful thought struck her. "S'posing," she said, "just supposing — no one comes."

Chapter 9

The Mr. Crumbs Christmas Bazaar

They were up extra early on Saturday morning. Ben, Emily, and Sanjay went straight to the school hall to put the finishing touches to the tables and help set out the refreshments.

Laura went to see to Mr. Crumbs and help Mrs. Cox get him ready for the pony rides he was going to give at the bazaar.

He immediately sensed the excitement,

and they had trouble getting him to stand still while Laura painted hoof oil on his hooves to make them shiny.

Then he tried to eat the tinsel they were attaching to the browband at the top of his bridle.

"He probably thinks he's going to a horse show," Mrs. Cox chuckled, as they entwined red and green ribbons into his mane and tail. "We used to enter him with the children when they were young."

Laura changed her clothes and packed some hay and his water bucket in a bag, along with plenty of carrots for treats during the day.

Then she mounted up and leaned forward to give Mr. Crumbs a hug. "You're so smart. You're a real Christmas pony today."

Mrs. Cox led him along the road since

Laura had only ever ridden him in the field. Laura looked around her and, once again, was amazed at how different — how beautiful — the world looked from up on his back.

When they reached the school she was relieved to see lots of people waiting to go in. And a line had already formed at the sign they'd put up for the pony rides.

"Isn't he beautiful?" said one little girl, as they approached.

"I've got one dollar," said a boy. "So I can have two rides."

Mrs. Cox smiled. "I can see I'm going to be very busy today."

Laura dismounted and got Mr. Crumbs some water. Then she gave him a special hug. "I love you, Mr. Crumbs. Be a good boy today."

Hanging over the entrance to the hall

was Sanjay's masterpiece, a huge banner that read:

THE MR. CRUMBS CHRISTMAS BAZAAR
10 o'clock today

Inside, the hall looked incredible with all the decorations up and the tables piled high with goods. Even though she'd seen it almost finished the night before it still took Laura's breath away.

"Is everyone ready?" she asked.

Everyone nodded or called out yes from behind their tables.

"Okay. I'll open the doors." She took a deep breath. "The bazaar is now open," she declared.

The day passed in a haze of activity. All the children in the school must have come — and brought their parents.

All the bride dolls and Santas sold very quickly. Laura noticed that several adults who bought the dolls quickly hid them under their coats or in their bags — they were obviously Christmas presents.

Every time she looked up, she could see Mr. Crumbs going past the window with yet another child on his back. He really looked as though he was enjoying the company and all the attention.

Rebecca, who was in Laura's class, won the candy by guessing how many were in the jar. And the butcher's wife guessed the correct weight of the Christmas cake.

The raffle was an incredible success and made a hundred and two dollars. Mr.

Crumbs himself made twenty-five dollars. He could have made much more, but Mrs. Cox kept the number of rides down to fifty and made sure he had regular breaks.

There wasn't much left by the time they finally closed the doors. And all that remained on the refreshment table were empty plates and a couple of tea bags.

Ben went to help Mrs. Cox take Mr. Crumbs home and settle him in for the night while the rest of them cleaned up.

"Well done," said Miss Featherstone. "That was a big success. Do you think you've raised enough money?"

"We haven't counted it all yet," said Laura. "But thank you so much for helping and for arranging for us to use the hall."

"That's all right — I admire you for

what you're doing," said Miss Featherstone. "As I love horses myself, I can understand why you want to keep Mr. Crumbs — he's a beautiful pony."

"I don't suppose there's anywhere to keep him here?" said Laura. "A field behind the school, maybe? Everyone at school loved him today."

"I'd love to help, but I'm afraid it's impossible. We can't keep Mr. Crumbs on school property," said the teacher. "But I've been around horses for most of my life, so when you do find somewhere, if you need a hand with anything, I'd be glad to help."

"Thanks," said Laura. "That's great." Now they had someone to go to for advice. And maybe Miss Featherstone could teach Emily and Sanjay to ride, and even help Laura and Ben improve their skills.

It was quite late by the time they got home, but Ben wouldn't go to bed until they had counted all the money. They'd made an incredible five hundred seventy-eight dollars and fifty cents profit. When they added the money to what they'd already saved, they had six hundred eighty-three dollars and seventy-six cents. Almost enough for six months' keep.

Laura tumbled into bed, exhausted. But she knew she wouldn't sleep, her mind was too active. They were almost there — if only they could find somewhere to keep Mr. Crumbs. If only someone would read one of their ads and call about a field and shelter for him.

They were bound to . . . it would happen next week . . . their luck was turning after all.

Chapter 10

Christmas Eve

School let out for Christmas on Wednesday, and the four friends concentrated their efforts on finding somewhere to keep Mr. Crumbs. The success of the bazaar had renewed their enthusiasm. They looked everywhere — asked everyone they could think of. They asked at the City Council, the train station — any place they thought could possibly have any land.

But there was nothing. And nobody phoned about their ads.

"We're surrounded by fields," said Laura. "I can't believe there's not one we can use for Mr. Crumbs. Not even one he can share."

So they started looking farther away. The one place they found was the riding stables over at Westhorpe. But they only did full board at a hundred dollars a week. Even Laura agreed that was impossible.

By Christmas Eve, they were feeling very low. They'd never dreamed it would be so hard to find Mr. Crumbs a new home. And Mrs. Cox was leaving for Australia in two weeks. Time was running out.

At lunchtime it started snowing, and

everyone felt even more depressed — except for Emily. "We'll be able to earn more money now, snow shoveling," she explained.

The snowstorm didn't last long, but it was heavy and covered everything in a soft white blanket.

They decided to go and take care of Mr. Crumbs a bit earlier that afternoon, to groom him and put his blanket on before it snowed again.

They trudged wearily up to his field. Mr. Crumbs didn't hear them approach as he usually did because their footsteps were muffled by the snow. He was standing there looking really dejected.

"He's probably missing the goats," said Ben. "Maggie took them down South with her two days ago."

"Plus, he senses that something's wrong,"

said Laura. It broke her heart to see him like this.

At the sound of their voices, Mr. Crumbs pricked up his ears. He tossed his head, whinnied loudly, and trotted over.

Sanjay put on his halter and gave him some diced apple. Then he led him over to the stable.

Laura started to pick out his hooves with the hoof pick while Sanjay went to fill his feed bag. Ben took Emily to get his stable rug because it had gotten so cold.

"We've made our seven hundred dollars," Laura told Mr. Crumbs. "Seven hundred two dollars and thirty-four cents to be exact. Ben put Saturday's pocket money straight into the bank today."

She got the grooming brushes and started brushing the pony's golden coat with the brush. He turned to look at her, and she felt his warm, sweet breath on her face.

"All we need now is somewhere to keep you," said Laura, trying to sound cheerful. "There's probably somewhere really obvious that we just haven't thought of yet."

She moved in front of him. Mr. Crumbs's dark velvet eyes were sad. "I can't fool you, can I?" she said. "You're too intelligent. You know things aren't looking too hopeful right now."

Mr. Crumbs rested his head on Laura's shoulder.

Laura put her arms around his neck, and they stood there for a while, enjoying each other's warmth and comfort.

"Don't worry, I won't let you go," said Laura.

"You might have to," Ben warned her, as he and Emily came back with the stable rug. "There just isn't anywhere to keep him."

Laura didn't answer. She knew she'd burst into tears if she did.

It was snowing quite heavily again by the time they left Mr. Crumbs. They trudged homeward and paused outside Ben and Laura's house to say good-bye. "Looks like Mom and Dad are still out Christmas shopping," said Ben. "The car's not here —" He stopped as they heard a shout.

"It came from Mr. Jakes's house," said Emily. "What's he up to?"

"Oh, I can't be bothered with him right now," said Ben.

"Just ignore him, Emily," said Laura wearily.

The shout came again.

"He's calling for help," said Sanjay.

They immediately ran over to see Mr. Jakes lying in his driveway.

"I slipped on the snow," he cried. "I think I've broken my leg."

They rushed to help him. His head was bleeding, and his leg was twisted in the strangest position. "Can you sit up?" asked Emily, bending down to him.

He waved her away. "Don't bother with me. Get help for the dog."

They all looked at each other in surprise. They didn't know he had a dog.

"What dog?" Laura asked.

"In the barn," he said. "She's giving birth — but she's having trouble. Get some help."

The four children raced to the barn. The door was open and they cautiously peered inside.

As their eyes became accustomed to the darkness, they could see a black dog lying on a bed of straw. And there was more. . . .

"Look, in that cage over there," said Laura, as they ventured in. "It's an owl."

"And look, over there," said Sanjay. "A rabbit — and a pigeon."

Something scurried to a corner of the barn. "A fox," gasped Ben. "And his leg is bandaged."

An elderly looking ginger cat came to greet them and rubbed against their legs.

"It's the one you saw coming in here, Emily," said Laura.

Something was snoring in a box under a table, and a chicken squawked from the other side of the barn. "And that's the chicken I heard," said Emily.

"What are they all doing here?" said Sanjay, as the owl winked at him with its one eye.

"I don't know." Laura kneeled down beside the trembling dog. "But look at this poor dog. She really needs help."

Ben looked outside. "The back door of the house is open. I'll go and phone for some help."

Laura went back to see Mr. Jakes. He was trying to drag himself up the driveway on his backside.

"You shouldn't move that leg," said Laura.

"Don't worry about me," snapped the old man. "I told you to get help for the dog."

Ben appeared. "It's all under control. I've phoned for an ambulance for you," he told the old man. "And I've called a vet for the dog."

"What?" said Mr. Jakes. "I'm not going to the hospital. My animals need me — I can't just leave them. And I can't afford to have a vet come out. They charge a fortune for a house call — and for an emergency. And this is both. Can't you get your parents to help or something?"

"Our parents are out," said Ben. "And we can't waste time trying to find someone who just might be able to help. That dog needs a vet," he added firmly. "And she needs one now."

"And we'll look after the animals if you have to stay in the hospital," said Laura.

"You? You're just kids," said Mr. Jakes. "I'm not letting you anywhere near my animals."

Sanjay put his hands on his hips indignantly. "We're not 'just kids.' And we know all about looking after ponies — so your smaller animals and a couple of birds shouldn't be a problem."

Ben took out his notebook and pencil. "We know about cats, dogs, and chickens. Just tell us what to do with the others."

Mr. Jakes winced in pain. "I suppose I don't really have a choice — like this. I'll have to trust you." He quickly told them how to care for the owl, rabbit, fox, and pigeon. The hedgehog — which was what the snoring from the box under the table was — was hibernating and wouldn't need any attention. "You will treat them kindly, won't you?" he added.

"Of course we will," said Emily.

"But I've got no money at all to pay the vet," said Mr. Jakes. "I bet it will cost at least a hundred dollars — maybe more."

Laura looked down at him. His eyes were moist. And it wasn't from the pain — he really cared about his animals. He wasn't a horrible man like they'd thought. She shifted her feet. "We've got some money," she said quietly.

"But that's for Mr. Crumbs," said Ben.

Chapter 11

Give the Kids a Chance

Mr. Jakes was just being carried into the ambulance when the vet arrived. The decision to pay for him with some of their money hadn't taken long to make. They couldn't let the poor dog suffer, and they knew it was important to move fast.

And as Emily said, they'd have a week and a half after Christmas to earn some more money. "We'll just have to work extra hard. At least we can do some snow shoveling."

"It'll mean less time to look for somewhere for Mr. Crumbs to live," said Ben. "Especially now we've got to look after Mr. Jakes's animals as well."

They waited silently at one side of the barn until the vet called them over. He explained that one of the puppies had died and was blocking the way for the others to be born. "It's a good thing you called me when you did," he told them.

"Is the dog all right?" Laura asked him anxiously.

"She's fine now." He smiled at them. "And how's this for a Christmas present?" He pointed to two tiny puppies suckling from their mother.

"Oh, they're so sweet," said Emily.

"The black one's a boy, and the sandy one's a girl," said the vet.

"We should think of names for them," said Ben.

Laura looked at the contented trio on the straw. There was something special, magical even, about a birth on Christmas

Eve. "How about Mary and Joseph?" she suggested.

"Great!" they all agreed.

Later, the hospital called to say Mr. Jakes had to stay. Dad was home and he offered to drive the children there so they could tell him about the puppies.

They arrived just as Mr. Jakes came back from being x-rayed. He didn't look so fierce, lying in a hospital bed. His leg was badly broken, and he had to have an operation that evening.

"Your dog's fine," Laura told him. "She's had two beautiful puppies."

"We've called them Mary and Joseph," said Emily. "Oh — unless you'd rather call them something else."

"No, they're good names," said Mr. Jakes. "But the money for the vet," he turned toward Laura's dad. "I can't repay you."

"I haven't paid anything," said Dad. "What have you kids been up to?"

"It's all right, Dad. We're paying," said Ben. "The vet's sending his bill after Christmas."

"You're paying?" said the old man. "How?"

Between them, the children explained about Mr. Crumbs, including the reason they'd wanted to use his barn.

"Why didn't you say that was why you needed the barn?" he asked.

"You didn't exactly give us a chance," said Sanjay.

"No, you're right. I'm sorry. But I get very twitchy about anyone going near the barn, because of the animals," said Mr. Jakes. "Some of them have already been poorly treated. The dog was thrown out onto the street by her owner — presumably because she was pregnant. And the fox was injured by boys throwing stones at it."

"We're not like that," said Ben indignantly.

"I know that now. And I'm so grateful to you for using your hard-earned money for my dog." Mr. Jakes shifted uncomfortably in the bed. "But what about your pony? Where are you going to keep him?"

"We can't find a place," said Laura sadly.

"Well, providing you're going to look after him yourself, he can live in my barn," said Mr. Jakes. "I won't charge you anything."

"Wow!" said Laura, Emily, and Sanjay together.

"It wouldn't be any good," said Ben

quickly. "He's got to have at least an acre of field, and you've got hardly any garden."

"The field out back belongs to me," said Mr. Jakes. "I bought it along with the farm cottage and the barn — it took all of my money. There was this donkey, you see — but she died before I could get her here. . . ." His eyes misted over. "But it would be perfect for your pony."

Laura couldn't believe it. Mr. Crumbs would be living just next door! "Oh, that's wonderful! Thank you so much, Mr. Jakes."

"Now easy," said Dad. He'd gone quite pale. "You're going a bit fast here."

"But you promised!" Laura and Ben shouted at once.

"I didn't promise — I said I'd think about it," said Dad. "But I didn't really think —"

"You didn't think we could do it, did you?" said Laura. "But we have. We've got six months' money in advance, and now we've got somewhere to keep him."

"Only we haven't got six months' money now," whispered Emily. "Not once we've paid the vet."

"Yes, we have," said Ben. "If we don't have to pay rent, then we've got plenty of money." He whipped his calculator out.

"Without rent — for six months we only need about four hundred and sixty dollars to keep Mr. Crumbs."

"And even if we have to pay the vet a hundred dollars, we've still got six hundred and two dollars and thirty-four cents left," said Laura.

"Oh, come on, give the kids a chance," said Mr. Jakes. "What they've achieved is incredible. What are you worried about?"

"Money — I can't afford to bail them out if they get into trouble. I've only just started up my business. And I'm sure Emily's mom —"

Mr. Jakes beckoned Dad closer and whispered something to him.

As Dad listened, a smile gradually spread across his face.

"What?" said Laura.

Chapter 12

The Christmas Pony

"Merry Christmas, Mr. Crumbs." Laura took out the carrot-shaped Christmas present.

"That's a little obvious, isn't it?" Emily laughed.

Mr. Crumbs pawed the snow-covered ground impatiently as Laura unwrapped it for him. It was a perfect Christmas day. Snow on the ground, but bright and crisp.

And best of all — they now had their very own pony.

"I couldn't be more pleased," said Mrs. Cox. "Fancy Mr. Jakes coming through like that. I'd never have thought of asking him."

"He's actually quite friendly when you start talking to him," said Ben. "And he knows a lot about animals."

"And he doesn't look so old when he's not scowling," said Sanjay. "He's only been retired for a few years."

Mr. Jakes had told them how he'd been taking in lost, unwanted, and injured animals since he'd moved there six months ago. He'd tried to keep it a secret because he didn't want people poking around and frightening the animals.

"Did you find out what Mr. Jakes whispered to your dad to make him give in?" asked Sanjay.

"He pointed out that a pony and carriage could be used for weddings," said Ben. "Dad's already worked out that it would be much cheaper than a second vintage car — which was what he was aiming toward."

"Mr. Crumbs used to love pulling our old carriage," said Mrs. Cox. She stroked the pony's nose. "You'd enjoy doing that again, wouldn't you, Crumbs? Lots of company, lots of exercise."

"I still can't believe it," said Emily. "Mr. Jakes was the last person I thought would have helped us. I thought —" She gave a giggle. "I thought he was a bank robber."

They all laughed.

Ben fastened the pony's stable rug on

him to keep him warm and dry out in the snowy field.

"And we don't have to pay any rent, so we won't have to work so hard." Laura stroked Mr. Crumbs's soft nose. "We'll be able to spend more time with you."

Mr. Crumbs gave a soft whinny and tried to get in her pocket for the second hidden carrot.

Laura took it out and unwrapped it for him. They'd already decided to hold a Christmas bazaar every year and have a booth at the village summer fair. They still had to earn money, not only for Mr. Crumbs's keep but because they wanted to help with Mr. Jakes's rescued animals, too.

Laura gave Mr. Crumbs another piece of carrot.

"He'll love it in the barn with all the

other animals," said Sanjay. "Especially when our dads have built his stall at one end."

"And I can leave without worrying now," said Mrs. Cox. "Knowing that Mr. Crumbs will be happy and well cared for. But I'm going to miss you all."

"We'll write to you — often," said Laura. "And let you know how Mr. Crumbs is doing."

The pony crunched on his carrot with his ears pricked, listening to them.

He gave a little snicker as Tiggy appeared and rubbed herself against his back leg. Then he put his soft muzzle into Laura's hand to see if he'd missed any bits of carrot.

She kissed him on his nose. "And you know what else, Crumbs? Tiggy's coming, too. Mr. Jakes said it's okay."

Ben patted Mr. Crumbs's neck. "Mr. Jakes is all right. He's just one of those people who gets along better with animals than with humans."

"But he wants us around there," said Laura. "And most important of all . . ." she reached up and whispered in Mr. Crumbs's ear, "he wants you."

Mr. Crumbs whinnied softly and rested his head on Laura's shoulder.

"Merry Christmas, everyone," said Laura, hugging him. "And a very special Merry Christmas to you, Mr. Crumbs — our very own Christmas Pony."